W9-CEJ-264

Christmas Magic!

by Lauren Cecil

SCHOLASTIC INC.

No part of this publication may be reproduced, stored in a retrieval system, or transmitted in any form or by any means, electronic, mechanical, photocopying, recording, or otherwise, without written permission of the publisher. For information regarding permission, write to Scholastic Inc., Attention: Permissions Department, 557 Broadway, New York, NY 10012.

ISBN 978-0-545-46756-8

© 2012 MGA Entertainment, Inc. LALALOOPSY™ is a trademark of MGA in the U.S. and other countries. All logos, names, characters, likenesses, images, slogans, and packaging appearance are the property of MGA. Used under license by Scholastic Inc. SCHOLASTIC and associated logos are trademarks and/or registered trademarks of Scholastic Inc.

12 11 10 9 8 7 6 5 4 3 2 1

12 13 14 15 16 / 0

Designed by Angela Jun
Printed in the U.S.A.
First printing, September 2012

40

It was the holiday season in Lalaloopsy Land. Holly Sleighbells was so excited she could hardly sit still.

"I can't wait for Christmas this year!" said Holly. Then she made a list of everything she had to do before Christmas.

☆ make cookies
☆ write cards
☆ decorate tree
☆ wrap presents
☆ hang stocking
☆ go caroling

Holly looked for her cookie recipe, but couldn't find it. "That's okay," said Holly. "I think I remember how to do it." Holly was just too excited to wait!

little while later, Mittens Fluff 'n' Stuff and Swirly Figure Eight visited Holly.

"You're just in time for cookies," Holly said. But when she took the cookies out of the oven, they looked terrible!

"Want us to help you make another batch?" asked Mittens.

"That's okay," Holly answered. "I'll do it after I send Christmas cards."

Mittens and Swirly thought Holly might need help. So they went to Crumbs Sugar Cookie's house.

"We want to surprise Holly with some cookies," Swirly said.

"That's super-sweet!" Crumbs said. "Christmas cookies are my specialty."

"Making cookies with friends is really fun," said Swirly as she mixed together the ingredients.

When the cookies were done, Mittens and Swirly dropped them off at Holly's house.

After Holly finished writing Christmas cards, she went outside to mail them.

"How magical!" Holly squealed when she saw the cookies. "These are just what I need. Now I can start decorating my tree!"

Holly pulled one end of a long strand of twinkle lights, but it was a tangled mess. As she tried to untwist them, she got stuck.

"Uh-oh!" Holly cried. She lost her balance and fell right into her Christmas tree.

Luckily, Mittens and Swirly were nearby and heard the crash.
"Holly!" cried Swirly. "Are you okay?"
"Do you want us to help you clean up?" asked Mittens.
"No, thank you," Holly said. "I can do it myself."

"Are you sure?" Swirly asked. "Friends are supposed to help each other out."

"I'm sure," Holly insisted.

Swirly and Mittens knew Holly was trying to do too much on her own. So they went to see Spot Splatter Splash.

"Could you help us make Holly some new ornaments?" Swirly asked.

"Of course," Spot said. "We can all make them together."

"Making things with your friends is so much fun," Swirly said. "Holly doesn't know what she's missing."

After Holly finished cleaning her living room, she was tired. "I'll just take a nap," said Holly. "Then I'll make some new ornaments."

A little while later, Swirly and Mittens tiptoed into Holly's house.

As Holly slept, the girls quietly hung the new ornaments. Then they snuck back out the door.

Holly woke from her nap and yawned. Then she saw her tree and rubbed her eyes.

"Am I still dreaming?" she asked. "My tree looks great! It must be magic."

Now Holly was ready to get started on her next task: wrapping presents.

Right away, Holly ran out of tape. She thought about going to get more, but she was just too excited to wait.

"I think I can use glue instead," said Holly.

But the glue just made a big gooey mess!

Mittens and Swirly saw Holly as she went out for tape.
"I have a feeling something else has gone wrong," said Swirly.

16

Inside Holly's house, Swirly and Mittens saw the mess.
They quickly cleaned up and rewrapped the presents for Holly.

When Holly got home, she saw how wonderful everything looked. "It happened again!" cried Holly. "This Christmas is more magical than any other!"

Holly read the next task off her list. "Hang stocking," she said. "Well, that should be easy!"

* make cookies
* write cards
* decorate tree
* wrap presents
* hang stocking
* go caroling

fter Holly hung her stocking, she noticed a loose thread on the toe.

"I can fix that," Holly said as she tugged on the string. At first it didn't come out. So she tugged harder. Soon, the entire stocking had unraveled.

olly was about to start crying when she heard voices coming from outside.

She opened her door and found Harmony B. Sharp, Swirly, and Mittens singing a Christmas carol.

"We thought you could use some holiday cheer!" Mittens said after their song.

"And we brought you a special present," Harmony said.

"This stocking is perfect!" Holly said. "How did you know it was just what I needed?"

"**W**ould you like to come caroling with us?" Mittens asked.
"Of course I would!" Holly said. "It's the last thing I have to do before Christmas."

"**P**erfect!" Swirly added.
   They caroled throughout Lalaloopsy Land and had a joyous time.

Suddenly, snowflakes began falling from the sky.
"Looks like it'll be a white Christmas after all," Holly said.
"How magical!" Mittens added.

© MGA © MGA © MGA